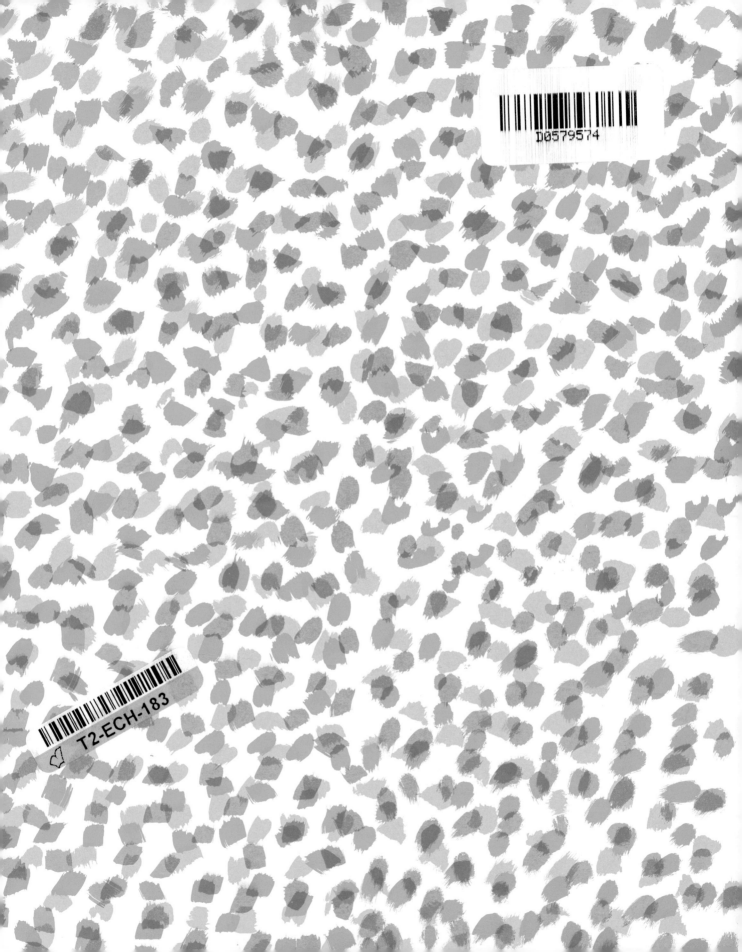

There are lots of umbrellas inside this book. Can you help us find them all?

Joe

Brian

Izzy

Grace

Under the Love Umbrella

Davina Bell
with illustrations by
Allison Colpoys

SCRIBBLE

*If you've ever felt
lonely or lost or alone, here is
a book for you with love.
Davina x x*

*To dear Ian, Diana & Sally Colpoys,
Thank you for always making me feel
like I am under your love umbrella.
Love, Al x x*

The illustrations in this book were made with ink and pencil and digitally assembled.

First published by Scribble, an imprint of Scribe Publications in 2017
Reprinted 2017 (twice), 2018 (twice), 2019
This edition published 2020

18–20 Edward Street, Brunswick, Victoria 3056, Australia
2 John Street, Clerkenwell, London, WC1N 2ES, United Kingdom
3754 Pleasant Ave, Suite 100, Minneapolis, Minnesota 55409 USA

Text © Davina Bell 2017
Illustrations © Allison Colpoys 2017

Printed and bound in China by Imago

9781925321265 (Australian HB edition)
9781925228205 (UK HB edition)
9781925228977 (UK PB edition)
9781947534971 (North American edition)

Catalogue records for this title are available from the
National Library of Australia and the British Library.

scribblekidsbooks.com

Up in the sky, among the stars
There's something you might not see...

But over your head and just above
There's an umbrella of my love

To show it's you I'm thinking of
Wherever you might be.

In deepest dark...

When big dogs bark

Or waves crash loud
Is that a shark?

When friends won't share
And things aren't fair

There's always
my love umbrella.

You're feeling shy
You don't know why?

Forgot your hat
You want to cry?

Remember...

I am standing by
Because of our love umbrella.

When everything is strange and new

On days when you need super glue

There's so much room here just for you
Under my love umbrella.

Bad dream

Lost tooth

Smashed toy

Big worry

Your pants are wet

You're meant to hurry

It disappears in a big old flurry
Under the love umbrella.

Whatever you fear,
come close, my dear

You're tucked in safe for always here

And I will never not be near
Holding our love umbrella.

In every weather

It's us together

My love for you goes on forever

Be still, breathe deep
Wherever you sleep

You're under my love umbrella.

Up in the sky, among the stars
There's something you might not see

But over your head and just above
There's an umbrella of my love
To show it's you I'm thinking of...

Wherever you might be.

Who's under your Love Umbrella?

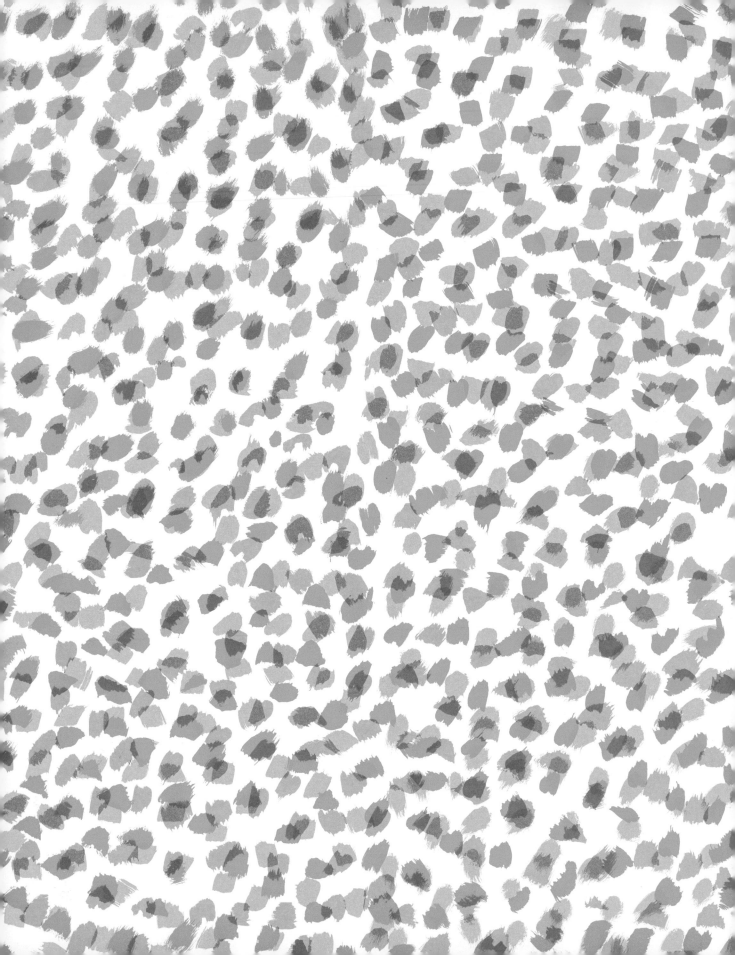